JIM HENSON'S MUPPETS

IN

Piggy Can't Wait!

A Book About Patience

By Eleanor Freemont • Illustrated by Tom Brannon

GROLIER

Piggy was excited. Today was the day her Aunt Wiggy was coming to visit. She was going to stay for two whole months. Aunt Wiggy lived far, far away, so Piggy hardly ever got to see her.

Aunt Wiggy arrived and got settled. Then she said, "Piggy, I have something special for you." She handed Piggy a box wrapped in pretty blue paper.

Piggy tore the wrapping off the box.

Inside were four little pots. In each one was a teeny-tiny little plant.

"Oooooh!" cried Piggy. "Thanks, Aunt Wiggy!"

"You're welcome," said Aunt Wiggy. "These plants are babies now, but they will grow nice and big. Then each one will have surprises for you."

"Surprises!" said Piggy. "I can't wait!"

"I'm afraid that waiting is exactly what you'll
have to do, my dear," said Aunt Wiggy. "You see,
plants need four things to grow: They need
water, plant food, sunlight, and patience—lots
of patience."

"I don't think I'm very good at being patient,"
said Piggy. "But I'll try."

So Piggy put the plants in the sunniest window and started trying to be patient.

The first day, she sat and watched the little plants for a whole hour. But they didn't grow at all.

Maybe, said Piggy to herself, *if I give them more water, they'll grow faster.* So she gave them lots and lots of water.

But they weren't any bigger by the next day. In fact, they looked a little droopy.

Maybe, said Piggy to herself, *if I give them extra plant food, they'll shoot right up.* So she gave them a very big drink of plant food.

But a few hours later, the plants looked even droopier.

"Oh, why don't they grow faster?" said Piggy that night. "I want my surprises!"

She looked at her plants, tapping her foot as she thought. "I know," she said finally. "Aunt Wiggy said they need sunlight. I'll give them some extra help."

So she set up her desk lamp right over them and switched it on.

The next morning, the plants looked very, very droopy indeed. In fact, they were so droopy that Piggy was worried about them. She waited until Aunt Wiggy came down for breakfast.

"Aunt Wiggy," said Piggy, "I've been trying to help my plants grow faster, but they don't look very happy. I gave them lots of extra water and plant food and light. Should I give them even more?"

"Oh, my goodness, Piggy," said Aunt Wiggy. "No, indeed!"

She gave Piggy's arm a pat. "You were very good at remembering the first three things your plants need. But I think you forgot about the last one—patience! Extra water and food and light won't make them grow any faster."

"Uh-oh," said Piggy.

"I think they'll be okay if you leave them alone for a while," said Aunt Wiggy. "But from now on, just give them a little extra patience."

"But I don't know how to give them patience," said Piggy.

"I'll tell you a secret," said Aunt Wiggy. "The best way to wait for something is to try not to think about it at all. Go and have fun. I'll take care of your plants for a little while."

"Thanks, Aunt Wiggy," said Piggy.

All day, Piggy tried not to think about her plants.

It was hard. The next day Kermit came over to play cards with her. Piggy wanted to jump up every half hour to see if her plants had grown. But she didn't.

The next day, she went on a picnic with Aunt
Wiggy. They had a very nice time, and Piggy only
thought about her plants two times all day.

When they got home that evening, Piggy
really wanted to look at her plants. But she didn't.
I have to be patient, she reminded herself.

As the days went by, Piggy thought more and more about the other things she was doing, and less and less about her plants. It became easier to stay away from them. *Aunt Wiggy is giving them water and food and light,* she said to herself, *and I'm giving them patience.*

A couple of weeks went by this way, until one weekend Piggy went to a sleepover at Skeeter's house.

As they crawled into bed, Piggy told Skeeter about her plants—and how hard it was to wait for the surprises.

"Wow," said Skeeter. "I know what you mean. I can't wait for anything either!"

When Piggy came home the next morning, Aunt Wiggy was waiting for her. "Piggy!" she said. "Your patience has paid off. The plants have grown. Come and see."

"Wow!" said Piggy. Each one of the plants had little flowers.

"These flowers will turn into cherry tomatoes. And these are peppers, these are beans, and these are cucumbers. Tomorrow, we'll plant them all in the backyard. Soon each plant will bear its own fruit."

"It'll be hard to wait for the tomatoes and peppers and beans and cucumbers," said Piggy, "but I'm getting much better at being patient."

For the next few weeks, Piggy waited patiently for the vegetables to get big enough to eat. She gave them just the right amount of water every day. Slowly but surely, they got bigger and riper—until at last they were just right.

On the last night of Aunt Wiggy's visit, they picked all the vegetables. For dinner Piggy's family had a wonderful salad.

"What do you think of your surprises?" Aunt Wiggy asked her.

"They're the best surprises I've ever tasted," Piggy said. "This is one salad that was really worth waiting for!"

Let's Talk About Patience

Sometimes we have to wait for things to happen. That takes patience. Piggy needed patience while she waited for her plants to grow. It isn't always easy to be patient, but as Piggy found out, some things are worth waiting for.

Here are some questions about patience for you to think about:

Have you ever had to be patient? What were you waiting for?

Was it easy or hard for you to be patient?

What things can you do to practice being patient?

Printed in the U.S.A.

ISBN 0-7172-8704-1